To..

Happy Halloween!

Love...

Prepare If You Dare

A Halloween Scare in BOSTON

Written by Eric James
Illustrated by Marina Le Ray

HOMETOWN
WORLD

Prepare, if you dare,
for a big **Boston** scare,
A tale of pure terror to whiten your hair,

A night full of sights that are best left unseen.
You ready? You sure?
This was my Halloween.

The werewolves howled loudly.
The moon shone so bright.
I stayed in my bedroom,
the curtains shut tight.

My heart started pounding,
my knees felt so weak,
But, being a brave kid,
I just **had** to peek.

I pulled back the curtains. My mouth opened wide.
An army of monsters had gathered outside!
They staggered and stumbled and lurched down the streets
With bags full of cookies and candy corn treats.

Emerging from sewers and houses and stores
Came creatures and critters with ravenous roars.
Then more came along from all over the state.
They filled up the streets at a dizzying rate!

From **Fenway,** the **North End,** and **Chinatown** too,
A mountain of monsters, the motliest crew,

All gathered together
for one **spooky** night,
To seek out the living
and give them a **fright.**

The thunder clapped loudly with terrible booms.
The witches dodged lightning and clung to their brooms.
The two-headed doggies tried chasing their tails,
And banshees let loose with their hideous wails.

The vampires hung out
on the street in their gangs,
And grinned, just to show off
their pearly white fangs.

The mummies moaned loudly and swayed side to side,
While FranKenstein stomped about town with his bride.

The **ogres** from Charlestown all hid out of view,
Then scared little children by shouting out "BOO!"
(These ogres were actually really nice guys,
But needed the screams to make Boston Scream Pies!)

A gaggle of **witches** arrived in the dark,
To play Witches' Baseball inside Fenway Park.
With broomsticks for bats and with balls made of lightning,
The game was quite thrilling, but also quite frightening!

The creepies were crawly, the crazies were crazed,
The **Beacon Hill** zombies had eyes that were glazed.
The **Somerville** ogres were ugly as sin,
With big bulging noses and warts on their chin.

The ghouls danced around but were lacking in soul,
The gargoyles could rock, and the headless could roll!
Although the whole spectacle seemed to spell doom,
I foolishly thought I'd be safe in my room!

EDGAR ALLAN POE

But then something happened
that made my heart jump.
From somewhere below me
I heard a big THUMP!

I froze for a moment, as quiet as a mouse.

Yes, I could hear noises from INSIDE THE HOUSE!

I put on my slippers

and pulled on my robe.

I shook like a leaf

but I don't think it showed.

Then, slowly but surely,

I crept down the stairs,

Preparing myself for the
biggest of scares.

My hands trembled wildly.
I opened the door.
I still shudder now
at the horrors I saw.
The stereo spat out
some hideous sounds
As dozens of monsters
jumped madly around.

The sight was horrific. It made my skin crawl.
These monsters were having their
Halloween Ball!

And right in the middle, one monster loomed tall,
The hairiest, scariest monster of all...

He turned round and saw me.
I fell to my knees.
"I'm not very tasty,
so don't eat me, please!"

He beamed ear-to-ear
and broke free from the huddle,

Ran over,
and gave me a...

BIG

MONSTER

CUDDLE!

"At last!
We have found you!" he said with a smile.
"From Hyde Park to Back Bay,
we've looked for a while.

BEST
COSTUME
IN
BOSTON

I ♥ BOSTO

"We came here to give you your wonderful prize."
He held up a trophy in front of my eyes.

"A prize? And for me?"

I replied with a grin.
"But what did I enter and how did I win?"
"You've won the first prize for the costume you're wearing!
It even scares me, and I'm tip-top at scaring!"

"This isn't a costume. I'm just dressed as me!"

"Exactly, the scariest thing you can be!

A small human child, with a cute button nose.

Your teeth are so shiny, you've only ten toes.

No hair on your face and no horns on your head.

The whites of your eyes are not glowing or red!

A bone-chilling costume! A horrible sight!

A worthy ensemble
for Halloween night!"

We partied together
until the moon set,
A Halloween night
that I'll never forget.

And next year I won't
want to hide in my bed.
The monsters won't scare me,

I'll scare

THEM

INSTEAD!

Written by Eric James
Illustrated by Marina Le Ray and Natalie Hinrichsen
Designed by Sarah Allen

Published by Hometown World,
an imprint of Sourcebooks Kids
P.O. Box 4410, Naperville, Illinois 60567-4410
(630) 961-3900
hometownworld.com
sourcebookskids.com

Date of Production: March 2021
Run Number: 5020472
Printed and bound in China (OGP)
10 9 8 7 6 5 4 3 2 1